CAROLINA SHOUT!

· ALAN SCHROEDER ·

PICTURES BY BERNIE FUCHS

New York Dial Books for Young Readers

To my dear friends, Larry and Mark

A.S.

To Zazie

B.F.

Ragtime and jazz enthusiasts will recognize the title of this book.
A sassy piece for solo piano, "Carolina Shout" was one of
James P. Johnson's earliest and most successful compositions.
Johnson (1894–1955) is perhaps best remembered for introducing
The Charleston in his 1923 musical show *Runnin' Wild.*

Published by Dial Books for Young Readers
A Division of Penguin Books USA Inc.
375 Hudson Street
New York, New York 10014
Text copyright © 1995 by Alan Schroeder
Pictures copyright © 1995 by Bernie Fuchs
All rights reserved
Designed by Atha Tehon
Printed in Hong Kong
First Edition
1 3 5 7 9 10 8 6 4 2

Library of Congress Cataloging in Publication Data
Schroeder, Alan.
Carolina shout! / by Alan Schroeder; pictures by Bernie Fuchs.—
1st ed.   p.   cm.
Summary: A young girl describes the music she hears in the cries of
various vendors on the streets of Charleston, South Carolina.
ISBN 0-8037-1676-1.—ISBN 0-8037-1678-8 (lib.)
[1. Charleston (S.C.)—Social life and customs—Fiction.
2. Cries—Fiction. 3. Afro-Americans—Fiction.]
I. Fuchs, Bernie, ill. II. Title.
PZ7.S3796Car 1995 [E]—dc20 94-17125 CIP AC

The illustrations were done in oils on canvas.

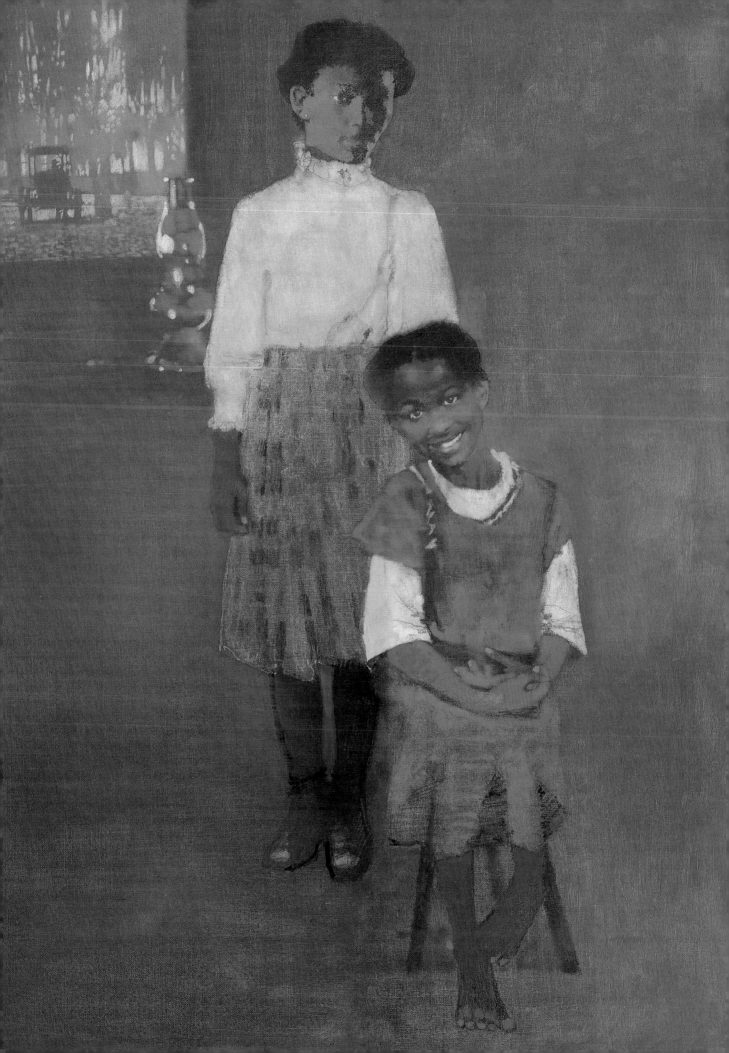

My name is delia

and I live in Charleston, South Carolina. One thing you ought to know about me. I love to dance, and wherever I go, I can hear music. My sister Bettina says she can't hear a thing when she goes outside—just the train whistle and maybe a mosquito if it starts buzzin' real close to her ear.

You know what I say to her? "You're just not listenin'. There's plenty of music, if you wanna hear it."

It's true.

I can hear music in the raindrops beating on the tin roof . . . in the sound of Mama's laughter . . . in the squeak of the rusty gate.

I can even hear it, late at night, in the croaking of the bullfrogs down near the marsh.

Have you ever really listened to a bullfrog?

Bettina hasn't. One night I brought a big fat one inside the house and put it on her bed and told it to croak. Only it didn't. I guess bullfrogs can be stubborn, just like people.

In Charleston if you want to hear music, all you have to do is hold still and listen. It'll come. You don't even have to go outside.

Early in the morning when I'm still in bed, warm under the covers, I can hear the creakety-creakety-creak of the wheels on the milk wagon and the wheezy old snuffle of the horse pulling it.

Then, real slow, the sun kisses the sky pink, and with a great throwing open of doors and shutters, Charleston begins to come alive. As I wash my face, I can hear, far away, the steam whistles on the river, and pretty soon, right outside the window, the clink of the milk bottles. It's not really music—not yet. But it's a start.

By the time I'm dressed, I can hear the carpenters working on the house next door. (They must get up awful early.) As they pound the nails into the rafters, they sing along, catching the rhythm with their hammers.

Whomp, bidda-bay!
Whomp, bidda-bay!
Come six o'clock,
we quit our day!

Whomp, bidda-bay!
Whomp, bidda-bay!
Six o'clock
we end our day!

Git in there, nail!

Farther down the road there's the song of the track workers.
I'm not supposed to get too near them, 'cause they're from the
state prison, but they have their own song. It goes like this:

Shack-a-lack
    -a-lack-a-lack.
Shack-a-lack
    -a-lack-a-lack!

Lay a rail,
snatch it back!

Shack-a-lack,
Shack-a-lack!

Lay that rail
    in wind and rain!
Every muscle I got's
    in pain!

Shack-a-lack,
Shack-a-lack,
Shack-a-lack-a-lack-a-lack!

At the morning market you can see the "Vegetubble Maumas" doin' their shopping, squeezing the tomatoes like they was squeezin' the cheeks of some little baby. All throughout the stands you can hear the vendors calling out their wares.

Red rose to-may-toes!
Green peas! Green peas!

Sweet as sugar—green peas!
Collards and greens,
Collards and greens!
Jui-ceee lemons!
  Come and gettum!
BLAAAACK—berries!

Listen close and you can hear the Waffle Man's cry. If you're standing in the right spot, you can smell his waffles a block away.

Get 'em hot,
  Piping hot,
Get 'em while they're
  good 'n hot!
Waf—ffffles here!

And then there's the Pepper-Sauce Man. He sells the hottest pepper-sauce in the city of Charleston. He also has the whitest teeth I've ever seen.

When you're passin' by this way,
When you're passin' this-a-way,
Keep a lis'nin' fo' ma call!

Pure Jamaica pepper-sauce!
Fresh red pepper-sauce!
Dat's all!

In Zigzag Alley you can hear the hopscotchers and rope jumpers makin' up the craziest rhymes. I can't believe Bettina doesn't hear *them*.

> *Chickama, Chickama,*
> *Craney-Crow,*
> *Went to the well to wash my toe!*
> *When I got back,*

My chicken was gone!
Packed her things and went to town!

Chickama, Chickama,
Now you're out!
Chickama, Chickama,
Don't you pout!

Papa says that times are hard, but you'd never know it here in Charleston. Even the chimney sweeps have their own song, and that must be the dirtiest, hardest kind of work of all.

> *Old Joe Cole,*
> *   good old soul,*
> *Sweepin' out*
> *   this dirty ol' hole!*
>
> *Sweep it out,*
> *   and do it fine—*
> *Or lady o' the house*
> *   don't pay a dime!*

My favorite place in Charleston is the harbor, where they sell boiled crayfish in stinky tin buckets. Day or night you can hear all kinds of music down at the waterfront. Even the Oyster Man has his own cry. I call it "The Shuckin' Song."

Shuckin' Time,
Shuckin' Time,
Two fresh pounds
Just a dime!

Get 'em fresh
In the shell!
Eat 'em here,
Just as well!

Shuckin' Time!

Yesterday the Oyster Man watched me dance. Then he gave me a free oyster. Took me all day to split it open. You never saw such a slimy thing in all your life! I told my sister Bettina to close her eyes and hold out her hand—I got a real special gift for her. When she saw what she was holdin', she hollered like I was killin' her. I expect we'll make up, but for now she's not talkin' to me.

The song I like best, though, is the one that's also the saddest. Every evening after the dishes are washed and dried, the Charcoal Man comes down the street with his buckets of coal. His voice is real raspy, like he's got coal dust in his throat and can't get it out. Maybe that's what makes his song so sad.

Char-coal! Dime a bucket!
Char-coal! Dime a bucket!

I walk in de moonlight,
I walk in de starlight,
I lay dis body down. . . .

Sometimes you hear this real long silence, and then he starts up again. Only this time he's farther away, and he drags out the word like it was made of rubber, only real sad.

Chaaar——coal.

Just hearing it makes your spine go chilly, and sitting next to the stove, watching the shadows play against the wall, I'm real glad to be indoors with Mama and Daddy and Bettina.

So I don't know what my sister means when she says she can't hear music when she goes outside. Way I see it, Charleston must be the most musical place on earth.

All you have to do is stand still and listen.

It'll come.

Author's Note

In the days before World War II, American street vendors relied upon short, rhythmic songs to call attention to their wares. Because these songs, or "shouts," were informal and varied from vendor to vendor, little effort has been made to collect them. This is regrettable, because they form a colorful and interesting part of our nation's cultural history.

Nevertheless, tantalizing scraps appear here and there. George and Ira Gershwin included three shouts in their opera *Porgy and Bess* (the Crab Man, the Honey Man, and the Strawberry Woman). A lively chapter on "Street Criers" appears in *Gumbo Ya-Ya*, a collection of Louisiana folklore compiled by Lyle Saxon, Edward Dreyer, and Robert Tallant (The Louisiana Library, 1945). Still another collection of shouts can be found in *The Book of Negro Folklore*, edited by Langston Hughes and Arna Bontemps (Dodd, Mead, 1958).

Many wonderful shouts, of course, were unable to find their way into this book. Among them: the Watermelon Vendor's Cry; the Knife Sharpener's Cry; the Hot Soup Song ("Peppry pot, all hot, all hot!"); the shouts of the Coffee Women and the Kindling Men; and the direct cry of the Ah-Got-Um Man ("Ah got um! Ah got um!"), who presumably sold a little of everything.

Each shout, by its very nature, reveals the personality of the crier; each, in its own way, is an authentic bit of American lore. Vendors like the Buttermilk Man, the Waffle Man, and the Coffee Women may no longer wander the streets and alleys of American cities, but their voices—their individual cries—should not be forgotten.